First American Edition 2017
Kane Miller, A Division of EDC Publishing

Text copyright © 2016 Chris Morphew, Rowan McAuley and David Harding
Illustration and design copyright © 2016 Hardie Grant Egmont
Illustration by Craig Phillips
Book cover design by Latifah Cornelius
First published in Australia by Hardie Grant Egmont 2016

For information contact:
Kane Miller, A Division of EDC Publishing
P.O. Box 470663
Tulsa, OK 74147-0663
www.kanemiller.com
www.edcpub.com
www.usbornebooksandmore.com

Library of Congress Control Number: 2016959847

Printed and bound in the United States of America
1 2 3 4 5 6 7 8 9 10

ISBN: 978-1-61067-659-5

THE DARK GIANTS

Cerberus Jones

THE GATEWAY

Kane Miller
A DIVISION OF EDC PUBLISHING

CHAPTER ONE

"Grawk!" Charlie bellowed through the bush. "Grawk! We've got more sausages for you."

"Forget it, Charlie," said Amelia. "If Grawk wanted to come, he'd have come by now. Plus, I think he can tell we don't have any sausages."

"Not *with* us," Charlie said to Amelia, then yelled again at the bush: "Obviously the sausages are in the fridge at the hotel, Grawk! You don't expect us to trek around in the sun with *raw meat*, do you?"

Amelia kept walking, picking the least-spiky

1

way through the undergrowth. "Maybe it's sausages that made him sick in the first place."

That would make sense. They'd last seen Grawk a week ago, when the hotel's old chest freezer had conked out and all the contents went bad. Dad had thrown it all onto the lawn at the back of the kitchen, and Grawk had slunk around and gorged himself.

The little alien creature had been acting strangely for weeks by then. Instead of being his usual funny, affectionate self, he'd started ignoring Amelia, then avoiding her, and then finally once or twice *growling* when she tried to talk to him. He'd never actually snapped at her, but after seeing him bring down a Hykryk time-shifter and bite the holo-emitter off her neck, Amelia wasn't about to push her luck.

Watching him wolf down three icy chickens, two legs of lamb, two catering packages of hamburger, and *eight pounds* of organic sausages, though, Amelia had wondered: *Maybe he was just hungry?*

She'd never imagined that he might need to eat so much. Poor thing – this whole time he'd been living with her, she'd been starving him! No wonder he was angry at her.

But how was she meant to know what a grawk needed to stay healthy? None of them did, and there was nobody she could ask. Somebody at Gateway Control might have been able to help, but Amelia was too scared to find out – she was pretty sure that "help" from Control would end up with Grawk being taken away and put down.

So maybe it was better for Grawk to stay out here in the bush. She missed him badly, but at least he was free.

Charlie wasn't having it, though. "You're being really slack, you know that, Grawk?" he bellowed

3

again. "It's Amelia's birthday today, you jerk!"

It was! Despite everything with Grawk, Amelia grinned to herself. Her actual birthday with an actual party at the hotel. She could hardly believe it – for the first time since arriving at Forgotten Bay, she was going to have her friends over.

"We'd better go back to the hotel," she said to Charlie. "I don't know how long we have before the Sophies get here."

"Oh, that's OK. You go," said Charlie, politely. "I'll just stay here in the bush a bit longer, getting bitten by bull ants and horseflies. Or maybe a red-bellied black snake. Or a funnel-web spider. Or a red-bellied black snake *and* a funnel-web spider."

"Charlie ..." Amelia said warningly.

"I mean, I'm not saying I'd rather die of venomous animal bites out here alone than see Sophie T. –"

"*Charlie ...*"

"I'm just saying it's a risk I'm willing to take."

"Charlie!"

"Well, come on, Amelia! Are you for real? *Both* Sophies at your party is bad enough, but asking Sophie T. to stay for a sleepover ..."

"Now who's being slack? It's my birthday, remember?"

"Yeah, but Sophie T.? *Sophie T.!*"

They might have had a real argument then, but instead they both froze as a tremor shook the ground beneath them. A flock of crows flew from the trees, crying out to one another in shock and disgust, "Gah! Gaah! Gaaaah!" The cicadas fell silent at once and the ants seemed to race along their trails twice as fast as usual.

Amelia and Charlie looked at each other and grinned before breaking into a sprint. Another arrival at the gateway! They crashed through the bush, scrambling over rocks and pushing through branches until they burst into the clearing around the groundskeeper's cottage.

But as they neared Tom's little house, Amelia felt the hair on the back of her neck prickle, and she slowed, approaching more nervously than usual. New alien guests were always interesting – educational, even – but that didn't mean they were *safe*. And since that time-shifter had messed around rewinding time over and over again, the wormholes that brought new visitors to Earth were behaving more erratically than ever. The disruption to his schedule was driving Tom crazy.

"I hope it's another blowback," puffed Charlie. "A good one, I mean."

"You would."

A blowback was when something accidentally slipped through a gateway – it happened now and then, when the wormholes were particularly un-stable or stormy. Grawk was the first blowback

Amelia and Charlie had come across, but he hadn't been the last. Two days ago, Tom had found the whole stairwell from his cottage down to the gateway filled with strange jellylike fruit. He'd gotten both kids to help him clear them out and dump them in the compost, and Charlie – against Tom's strictest orders – had tried one and discovered they were delicious (like lychees in lemonade) and made your eyes turn pink for an hour after.

Some of the other blowbacks had been less pleasant (a puddle of alien sewage), less useful (nearly seventy books, no pictures, all unreadable), and much less simple to clean up (a cloud of sticky foam belched up all over the stairwell walls and steps).

But from the noise up ahead, it didn't sound like a blowback this time. As they reached the front door – Charlie sniffing his way forward, in case it was sewage again – Amelia heard raised voices.

 7

"Go ahead," Tom said loudly. "Call Control – ask them yourself, but I'm telling you, there are *no* exceptions."

A mangled chirping came in reply, but by now Amelia was so used to listening to nonhuman versions of English, she could make out the words quite easily.

"But I'm a scientist! An exobiologist. Look at my papers – I'm here to study local earthling wildlife and how it interacts with a gateway. I *need* my equipment."

Amelia and Charlie peeped through the open doorway and saw Tom, his hands on his hips, standing his ground before a thin, orangey-gray creature that looked something like a centaur, with four legs on the ground and then an upright body with two arms. If, that is, centaurs weren't huge, noble horse people, but extremely scrawny little fox people.

James, Amelia's older brother, was keeping his head down, getting on with packing the alien's equipment into a storage box.

"That belongs to my university," the alien yipped. "It's highly sensitive, state-of-the-art – aaaargh! *Don't* tip that one upside down!"

"Sorry," muttered James, turning the object the right way up again.

"Give it to me," the alien snapped.

"No way," said Tom. "Nothing leaves this cottage that hasn't been registered ahead of time with Gateway Control. Since the Guild –"

"Do I look like Guild?" he shrieked.

"*Since* the Guild started rearing their heads again," Tom went on stubbornly, "*all* alien technology must either be registered with and approved by Control *before* leaving your home world, or left secure with us for the duration of your stay."

"Secure?!"

James taped up the lid of the box and offered the alien a clipboard and a pen. "Sign here, here and ... here, and keep this receipt here with you as proof of ownership."

Amelia watched as the alien signed over his equipment, clearly fuming. Then he tucked his hand into his fur, into what must have been some sort of pouch like a kangaroo's, and pulled out a small bronze cylinder.

"I have no idea what you expect me to do now," he seethed, attaching the cylinder to his neck. "Just *remember* the animals I see? Draw a sketch of them in the dirt with a stick? Perhaps I should –"

"I'll need to take that holo-emitter, too," said Tom, holding out his hand.

"What? You don't expect me to believe Control will let me stroll around on a non-stellar planet without a holo-emitter."

"You will need to wear one of *our* holo-emitters. All our images have been registered with Control, whereas yours ..."

"Fine!" The alien snatched off his holo-emitter and slapped it onto Tom's palm. "I'll wear yours. But if you think I'll submit to any more of Control's outrageous abuses of my liberty – an honest academic!"

Tom sighed heavily. "I'm going to need you to turn out the contents of that pouch ..."

The alien shrieked again, scandalized. He grabbed a holo-emitter from Tom's desk, fixed it to his neck and switched it on before Tom could finish his sentence. Immediately, the scrawny fox-centaur disappeared and a scrawny, orange-bearded man in a shabby corduroy suit appeared.

"I've never been so insulted in my life," the man snapped, his voice human now, but still high and furious. "Is there no courtesy at all in this wretched star system?" He walked past Amelia and Charlie, out the door, and up to the hotel.

"Another satisfied customer, Tom!" said Charlie.

Tom glowered at them both, but said nothing (it was Amelia's birthday, after all).

"Is it really Control's orders?" asked Amelia. "I mean, they don't even know about the canister the Guild tried to steal from –"

"And they don't need to," said Tom, glancing warily through his still-open front door. "They know the Guild were here, and that's more than enough for anybody to tighten border security."

"Yes, I know," said Amelia, "but –"

"Don't you have a party to go to?" Tom made *party* sound like it was a form of torture.

"Ugh, that's right," said Charlie. "Come on, then, Amelia. Let's get it over with."

"Oh, thanks a lot, Charlie. Happy birthday to me, huh?"

CHAPTER TWO

Amelia and Charlie had only made it halfway up the hill when Mrs. Flood's car crunched along the gravel driveway. Amelia waved at them from across the lawn and began to run, but neither Sophie F. nor Sophie T. noticed her. Through the car windows, Amelia could see that they were staring, white-faced, at the hotel.

"Ha! Look at them – they're totally freaking out!" Charlie grinned.

Amelia stopped and turned on him. "Don't you dare, Charlie Floros. I know you can't stand them, but the Sophies are my friends. And," she fixed him with a look. "It. Is. My. *Birthday*."

"Relax," said Charlie. "Everything will be great."

"I mean it, Charlie."

"So do I."

"Be nice," said Amelia. "Just until the party's over. Please?"

"I'll be better than nice." He smiled what he thought was his charming smile. "I'll be adorable."

Amelia groaned, but didn't waste any more time arguing with him. Instead, she hurried to the hotel, little bubbles of excitement making her skip up the steps to the big double doors. Her birthday was today, *and* she was having a party, *and* the Sophies were finally visiting her place for a change. OK, it *would* have been even better if Shani could've come. And sure, it was a pity that Sophie F. couldn't stay for the sleepover. And no, she wasn't confident about what Charlie's idea of "adorable" might be – but *still*, it was her birthday!

She let herself into the lobby, Charlie only a step behind, and saw Mrs. Flood standing under the old chandelier, looking around in wonder. The two Sophies were whispering together.

"Hi, guys," Amelia called. Not too loudly: Mum was busy at the reception desk, checking in the cranky alien in the corduroy suit, and several other guests (the usual mixture of holo-emitter-disguised aliens and unsuspecting humans) were milling around, wandering out from the dining hall or into the library or up the broad marble staircase on the right to the guest rooms.

Sophie F. turned at the sound of Amelia's voice and smiled back. "Happy birthday!"

Sophie T. smiled too, but then her eyebrows rose in surprise. "Are we early?"

"No," said Amelia. "Right on time. Thanks for coming."

"Oh, OK." Sophie T. frowned slightly. "Only – did we dress right?"

"What? Oh!" Amelia realized that both Sophies were wearing their good clothes: Sophie F. was in her new purple jeans and high-top sneakers, and Sophie T. was in a floaty, sky-blue sundress with a matching hairband, whereas Amelia ...

Amelia put a hand to her hair and felt a sort of bird's nest of knots and tangles and bits of leaf and twig. She looked down and saw the rip in her T-shirt, the scratches and dirt on her legs, and the hundreds of grass seeds on her socks. It was how she always looked after a day playing on the headland, but now –

"Cookie," said Mum, coming out from behind the reception desk and crossing the lobby. "Why don't you hurry and get changed while I take the Sophies through to tea?"

Amelia nodded gratefully and sprinted up the

left-hand staircase to the family wing of the hotel, determined to have the quickest wash and change in the history of parties. She dragged a brush through her hair, scrubbed her face and hands and knees with a boiling-hot washcloth, and pulled on the first dress she found in her drawer. The whole thing took less than ten minutes.

Ten minutes too long, though. As she pattered down the stairs and across the lobby to the dining room, she saw three things straightaway.

One: that Mrs. Flood was laughing and talking happily with Mum.

Two: that Mary and Dad had done a beautiful job setting up her birthday tea – a five-tier cake stand rose in the middle of the table, each level crowded with a different type of afternoon snack: tiny sandwiches on the bottom, tiny pink-and-chocolate cupcakes at the top, and scones and macaroons and sausage rolls in between.

17

And three: that Charlie was, from the looks on the Sophies' faces, being totally Charlie. She went over in time to hear him saying, "No, she's great. Seriously. I think all girls should be more like her. She has these awesome black leather hiking boots because she spends all day out in the bush working, and she has this amazing scar from her shoulder all the way down her arm, and –"

"Hello, Charlie," said Amelia quietly. "What are you talking about?"

"Oh, hey, Amelia." Charlie grabbed three tiny sandwiches at once and shoved them all in his mouth. "I's jus' tellin' the Soph's abou' –"

"About some ridiculous imaginary person he calls Lady Naomi," Sophie T. spoke over the top of Charlie's disgusting mumbling, and slanted him a withering look. "As if any *lady* would have a scar and work in the bush. What is she, a lumberjack?"

Amelia shook her head at Charlie, who raised

his hands helplessly. "What did I do?" he asked, swallowing his mouthful. "They were getting spooked about maybe seeing Tom tonight, and all I said was that apart from his missing eye, missing finger, gold tooth, limp and foul temper, he's basically a really nice guy, and *they* said this sounded like a horrible place to live –"

Sophie F. blushed, but Sophie T. held her chin high.

"And I was just trying to tell them all the other great things about living here –"

"– so you told them about Lady Naomi," Amelia finished for him.

"And every word was true." Charlie crammed two cupcakes in his mouth.

Sophie T. rolled her eyes, then decided to ignore him. As Amelia sat down beside her, Sophie T. said, "Well, you do have a lot of room here, anyway. You could easily get a rabbit *and* guinea pigs, if you wanted to."

"It's true," Amelia said. "But then I got a dog instead, remember? And I don't know if Grawk would get on very well with a rabbit."

"Yes, where is he?" asked Sophie F. "I want to see some of his tricks."

"Oh, uh ..." Amelia gulped and stalled for time by pouring a glass of vanilla milkshake from the pitcher on the table. "He's ..." She felt her friends watching her, concerned. "He's lost, actually."

"Oh, no," Sophie F. moaned. "You poor thing, when? You must be so worried."

"I am." Amelia was relieved. Even though her friends couldn't ever know the full story, they understood how she felt.

"Do you think he'll come back?"

"I hope so. Actually, that's where Charlie and I were when you arrived – out in the bush, looking for him."

"I don't blame you," said Sophie T. "If Arabella Moonglow went missing" – that was her white rabbit – "I wouldn't do anything else until I found her. I wouldn't even go to school."

There was a sad little pause in the conversation out of respect for Amelia's situation, and then Sophie T., who didn't like silence very much, patted Amelia's hand and said brightly, "I know! I can help you look for him tomorrow. We'll do an official search party."

"Thanks, Sophie." Amelia smiled. As much as Charlie thought Sophie T. was the biggest pain in the world, she really was a good friend. After all, anyone who *hated* getting dirty, thought all bugs and insects were repulsive, only ever wore the nicest clothes and yet *still* volunteered to go searching for an (alien) dog she'd never met before was pretty special.

Suddenly, both Sophies' heads swiveled around

as though magnetized and Amelia saw James walking towards them. She looked at her tall, gangling, super-sarcastic brother. What did the Sophies see that was making them blush and sit up straighter, she wondered.

"Hey, sis," he said, plonking himself down in the chair next to Sophie F. "Who're your friends?"

Amelia introduced them, and watched as Sophie F. shrank into herself and tried to become invisible, while Sophie T. flicked her blond hair back over one shoulder and made her eyes so big and focused on James that Amelia blinked twice as fast to compensate.

Luckily, before it got too weird, Mum signaled Mary in the kitchen. A minute later, Dad came out with an enormous sheet cake covered in lit candles. He was singing "Happy Birthday" and one by one, Mum, Mary, and the kids at her table joined in. Some of the guests did too – the human ones, anyway. The guests eating canned spaghetti with ice cream just observed, fascinated.

"Hip, hip," said Dad, setting down the cake in front of Amelia.

"Hooray!" shouted all the humans in the room.

Amelia took a deep breath and blew out her candles. And there were a *lot* of candles, spaced out unevenly all over the surface of the cake. By the time the last one sputtered out, Amelia was gasping.

Sophie T. did a quick count. "*Twenty* candles? But you're not twenty!"

Amelia grinned. "No, look – it's marking out the constellation of Sagittarius. My star sign."

Mrs. Flood gave Dad a funny look. "I thought you were a science man."

"I am," said Dad eagerly. "Astrophysicist, actually, and Sagittarius is a great set of stars to have in the sky for your birthday."

"Oh, really?" said Mrs. Flood, politely.

Mum smirked and started handing out spoons as Dad got going.

"Oh, yes!" he beamed. "Did you know, Sagittarius is one of the forty-eight constellations described by Ptolemy in the second century? And, even though we can't see it with the naked eye, it contains possibly the brightest star in our whole galaxy!"

"Uh-huh." Mrs. Flood nodded, unblinking, as Dad picked up the ginormous carving knife and suddenly stabbed it into the cake.

"Right *there*!" he exclaimed. "The Pistol Star! Hidden by cosmic dust, but a blue hypergiant so powerful it emits more energy in twenty seconds than our sun does in a whole year! Not only that but –"

"It tastes delicious, too," Mum finished smoothly.

"Eh?" Dad blinked, and then looked in surprise at the poor cake he'd just murdered. "What?"

"Amelia's birthday cake, dear," said Mum. "You were about to cut it up?"

Sophie T.'s eyes were as round as saucers. She had flecks of whipped cream on the front of her dress from the force of Dad's blow with the knife, but Sophie F. was giggling quietly to herself and looking at Dad with great interest.

"Well," said Dad, pulling the knife out and handing it to Amelia. "I think you're supposed to make the first cut."

Holding her breath, Amelia sliced into a corner without candles. What had Dad dreamed up this time? She sighed with relief as a perfectly ordinary slice of vanilla cake came away. It was such a large cake that everyone in the dining room had a slice. (Amelia talked very loudly to the Sophies, hoping they wouldn't notice the family of five who were squirting ketchup and mustard over theirs.)

Sophie F. had another slice of cake and Sophie T. said, "Hang on – presents!" and handed Amelia a gift bag. "It's from both of us."

Lifting out a framed photo of the three of them together, and a box of flavored jelly beans, *and* a new adventure book, Amelia thought this might be her best birthday ever. Back in the city, before they'd moved to Forgotten Bay, the Walkers' old apartment had been so small Amelia had always had her parties at the park, or ice skating, or the movies. Now, for the first time, she had a home that had room for everyone – her family, her best friend, her friends from school, and even random guests from other galaxies, if they wanted to. Even –

The room went silent. Someone had walked through the door, and this time it wasn't only the Sophies who turned to look.

CHAPTER THREE

A small, neat person walked quietly between the tables, making her way to Amelia. She was dressed in her usual drab uniform of cargo pants and a sleeveless T-shirt, but no one seemed to notice what she was wearing. Everyone was staring at her extraordinary face, at her sweep of long, jet-black hair, at the acrobatic elegance she compressed into just walking across the floor, and at the silver scar that twisted its way up her arm.

"Who is that?" Sophie T. gaped.

"That is Lady Naomi," said Charlie smugly.

"I told you she was cool."

Amelia hadn't thought for a moment that Lady Naomi would be at her birthday. Apart from the research that usually kept her out in the bush until well after nightfall, Lady Naomi preferred to avoid crowds, and Amelia could see why. For a very private person, it was almost impossible for her to go anywhere without attracting attention.

"Happy birthday," she smiled as she reached the table. "I hope I'm not interrupting."

"Never," sighed Sophie T.

"Do you want some cake?" said Charlie. "There's loads left."

"Maybe later," said Lady Naomi. "Right now, I was wondering if Amelia would like her present?"

"You got me a gift?"

"Well, not just me. I had the idea, but Ms. Rosby ordered the parts, and Tom did all the actual work."

Charlie goggled at Amelia in open jealousy.

"I hope you know when *my* birthday is," he said to Lady Naomi.

"It's not just for Amelia. You can all enjoy it together."

Mrs. Flood came over to the table and caught Sophie F.'s eye. "Time we were off, pumpkin."

"Oh, but Mum ..."

"No, come on. You've had cake and given Amelia her present, and now we have to go."

"Oh, could you possibly stay another ten minutes?" Lady Naomi asked. "I'm sorry to have left it so late, but I wanted to wait until it got completely dark. And we only need to go out to the lawn. You'll have to walk past anyway, won't you?"

"Well ..."

Amelia grinned at Sophie F. No one could resist Lady Naomi.

"Just ten minutes," Mrs. Flood agreed. "And then we really have to go."

Sophie F. didn't waste any time discussing it; she was already out of her chair and on her way to the door. Lady Naomi began to follow her and then realized that everyone in the dining room was still looking at her. She paused to check with Amelia. "If it's all right with you, birthday girl, everyone here can come too."

Amelia was confused now. What kind of gift could a hotel full of people enjoy at once? She couldn't wait to find out, and scrambled after Sophie F.

It wasn't until she was standing with Charlie and Sophie F. on the lawn that she noticed that Sophie T. wasn't there. She looked around and spied her friend standing on the hotel's verandah, underneath a lantern. "Come on, Sophie!" Amelia called. "Stand with us."

"I'm fine," Sophie T. called back. "I just don't want to get any dew on my new shoes."

"Oh, but there isn't any –"

Amelia stopped as Sophie F. touched her arm and whispered, "*She hates the dark.*"

Amelia blinked in surprise. She never would have guessed something so ordinary would bother Sophie T., but she tried hard not to show any reaction. She just nodded, then glanced over at Charlie. He had a triumphant gleam in his eye. Why did he have to have such sharp hearing?

Before he could do anything with this new information, Amelia said to Lady Naomi, "Where should I be looking? Is it here yet?"

"Yeah," said Charlie, thankfully changing tack. "Where is it, Lady N.? Did you get her Wonder Woman's invisible jet?"

Sophie F. snorted with laughter.

"Or did you get her a star? You can do that, you know: buy a star and name it whatever you like."

"True," said Amelia, "but you don't usually

order parts for a star or get Tom to work on it."

"Or invite everyone to see it," Sophie F. added.

"Well, what then?" said Charlie.

Lady Naomi appeared to ignore him, but called down the slope of the headland, "Ready when you are, Tom."

Amelia held her breath and peered into the darkness, wondering what Tom might be bringing up the hill. She was staring so intently that when the first explosion came, she gave a little scream.

"Whoa!" cried Sophie F., looking up as more explosions popped and thumped around her.

Amelia saw the sky bloom with color. All the guests from the hotel went, "Ooh!" together as one pinprick of yellow burst into a ball of blue sparks, and then they all sighed, "Ahh!" as stream after stream of red sparks shot up like pillars.

It was a brilliant show, and much more exciting than any fireworks Amelia had ever seen before.

Partly this was because these were so close she could feel the shock waves in her belly, and the ground reverberating through the soles of her feet. It was also because, as well as the usual green and white and red fireworks, there were a number of more ... peculiar ones.

A mauve firework puffed out like a chrysanthemum and then turned lime green, with hot-pink stars winking at the edge of each petal. A turquoise jet drew a sparkling oval in the sky, which then swam with dozens of orange fish. And as the grand finale, a golden comet squealed through the sky and wrote *HAPPY BIRTHDAY AMELIA* in letters so huge and bright, it took a couple of minutes for the image to fade from her retinas.

"That was amazing!" cheered Sophie F. "I've never seen anything like it!"

"I know!" crowed Charlie. "Who knew Tom

was a pyrotechnics expert? No wonder he blew off his finger and eye! I'm going to get him to teach me everything!"

Mrs. Flood waved and called.

"Oh, shoot, I've got to go," said Sophie F. "Thanks for having me, Amelia. That was the best!"

She hugged Amelia and then ran back to her mum and their car. Amelia smiled after her, still dazzled from the fireworks. In fact, it almost seemed as though she could see a dull-yellow glow out of the corner of one eye ...

She turned her head to see if the illusion would persist and got a nasty shock as something like a camera flash almost blinded her.

"What was that?" yelped Charlie.

Amelia blinked furiously, trying to recover her night vision, and pointed. "Over there somewhere."

"I see him," said Lady Naomi, and strode off towards the bush at the edge of the hotel's grounds.

Amelia looked back towards the hotel, torn. There was Sophie T., standing under the light, her arms crossed. She looked small and uncertain, and Amelia knew she should go back to her –

"Come on, Amelia!" Charlie called over his shoulder as he jogged after Lady Naomi.

She bit her lip, on the verge of letting Charlie go on without her, but then saw Sophie T.'s face break into a wide smile as James walked over to talk to her. Ignoring her guilty feelings, she turned and ran to catch up with Charlie and Lady Naomi.

They were almost at the edge of the hotel's lawn, where the grass gave way to the bush, when Amelia heard twigs snapping ahead of them.

"Stop right where you are," Lady Naomi called out, running now. But from the sound of crunching leaves and rustling bushes, whoever it was had no interest in taking orders.

"Right," said Lady Naomi grimly, "have it your way, then." She sprinted ahead with a sudden burst of speed.

Amelia heard a great commotion – more branches being snapped and the frantic scuffling of several feet, and then a yipping voice: "Get your hands *off* me!"

Amelia and Charlie pushed their way towards the ruckus. There was just enough light in the sky for them to make out two figures: one, obviously, was Lady Naomi. The other –

"It's the fox guy from Tom's cottage!"

"Why don't you have your holo-emitter on?" said Charlie. "You know Tom will tell Control."

"Never mind that," said Lady Naomi. "What was that device you were just using – and where is it now?"

"He's got a pouch," said Amelia. "That's how he smuggled it past Tom, I bet."

"A pouch?" said Lady Naomi, and there was a moment's more struggling and then a high, foxy scream of fury.

"You picked my pocket? You shameless barbarian! You ignorant savage! I'll have you know that I'm –"

"Be quiet," said Lady Naomi. "We don't care who you think you are. The only thing you need to tell us is what this device is, and what you were doing with it."

"It's nothing!" he barked. "Nothing you'd understand, anyway."

"Try us."

"Is it a scientific instrument?" said Amelia. "He said he's an exobiologist."

The alien sighed. "Fine. It's a multichannel bio-scanner. I use it to scan the environment for specific signs of life. Look: I can put in criteria – say, iron-based blood system, a single four-chambered heart, bipedal, put in the estimated size range of the animal and its usual body temperature and –" The machine gave an excited clockwork whir and a screen lit up with two pink dots. "See, there you are: two humans." He paused and then looked at Lady Naomi. "But not you ..."

"Right, good," she snapped. "A bio-scanner. And what are you doing with it?"

"Surveying the local environment, of course! That's my job. I'm a junior professor in gateway ecology – I've been studying how wormhole activity impacts the local wildlife."

"And does it?" said Amelia.

"Of course it does! All that magnetism, all those wormholes emitting strange gusts of atmosphere or blasts of alien dust. Imagine how many bacteria and fungi spores and different pollens are wafting onto Earth every time the gateway opens. Not to mention the muck we travelers bring through on our clothes and feet and fur. And what about blowbacks? Ever think about them?"

"Er, maybe ..." Amelia shuddered. She'd thought about Grawk, but never invisible things like diseases and pollution.

"Well, that's my area of study, and I think you can see why it's so important. I mean, I did my research before coming here – this is Australia, isn't it? How much trouble have you caused yourselves by bringing rabbits and cats and cane toads here? And they were at least native to Earth! Can you imagine how catastrophic it would be if just one breeding pair of Saulidean snapping yabbies got through? Or if –"

"All right, all right," said Charlie. "It's a good story, but we've heard those before. It doesn't prove that you're not up to something else."

"But Charlie –" Amelia didn't disagree with him, exactly, but she'd been hoping to find a way to ask if Foxy had seen any signs of Grawk before they'd burst in on him.

"Charlie's right," said Lady Naomi. "Even if your story is true, you ought to have registered your purpose for travel with Control as a science expedition."

"That process takes months! If I'd missed this wormhole, I would have had to wait over a year and a half before I could get to Earth. It was far better for me to travel as a tourist, and then later –"

"I can see your point," said Lady Naomi, "so I hope you can see ours, too. We are going to have to escort you down to Tom's so he can contact Control and –"

"Nope, sorry!" Foxy suddenly snatched his bio-scanner out of Lady Naomi's hand, and took off deeper into the bush. He might have been a scrawny little thing, but he was seriously fast on those paws.

Lady Naomi growled in annoyance. "Fantastic.

You two, tell Tom. I'll go and get this genius." She ran up the trunk of a leaning gum tree until she reached its first branch, ten feet above the ground, and looked for Foxy's path. "Got him," she murmured, and then sprang in that direction, disappearing immediately into the gloom.

"Wonder what Sophie T. would say if she'd seen *that*," said Charlie.

Sophie T.!

"Oh, no, I can't!" Amelia groaned. "She's –"

"You heard Lady Naomi. We've got to tell Tom *now*."

Feeling like the worst sleepover host ever, Amelia knew Charlie was right.

"Let's go," she said. Crashing their way back out of the bush, they turned away from the hotel, and headed down to Tom's.

CHAPTER FOUR

"Is Tom even down here?" said Charlie as they reached the clearing beyond the magnolia trees. "What if he went back up to the hotel after the fireworks to get some cake?"

"Now you ask!" said Amelia, but through Tom's lit window, she could see someone moving.

They crept slowly closer. It was always better to know who was in there before knocking, plus – although Amelia knew it was very bad manners – they'd learned a lot of really useful things by eavesdropping in the past.

"I know you can't go near it," Tom's voice drifted through the open window. "But there must be some way you can get rid of it. Throw it in the Nowhere, or –"

"Don't be ridiculous," said a second voice. "You've *seen* what happens when I even approach the thing. And even if I *could* take it from you, there's no telling what might happen if it entered the gateway. An energy source of that power – of that *nature*? The result could be catastrophic – we have no way of knowing what disaster we avoided when those Guild fools were stopped from stealing it."

"The canister," Charlie guessed in a whisper.

Amelia nodded – the canister that had been hidden at the hotel for over a century, until the Guild had come looking for it two weeks ago. The canister whose contents were so secret and dangerous that Tom refused to tell even Control about it. Worse: he'd *lied* to Ms. Rosby – the only agent at Control who was really on their side – and then he'd made Lady Naomi take it away and hide it somewhere so that not even *he* knew where it was.

"What do you expect us to do, then?" asked Tom, his voice rising. "Just *trust* that Lady Naomi's found a safe enough hiding place to keep the Guild from ever –"

"You might start by being a bit *quieter* about it," said the second voice, and before Amelia had time to wonder what he meant, two thin hands shot out through the open window, grabbed her and Charlie by the backs of their shirts, and dragged them into Tom's cottage. It wasn't comfortable, either: Amelia banged her knee hard on the windowsill.

"Hello, Leaf Man," said Charlie, as the pale, gaunt man dropped them to the floor. He stood back from them, shaking out the sleeves of his trench coat. He didn't look nearly strong enough to have hauled them through the air like that, but Amelia knew that behind his holographic disguise stood a powerful Keeper – a guardian of the gateways.

Tom glared at Amelia and Charlie as they got up from the floor. "When will you two learn to mind your own business?"

"We're *here* on business," Charlie retorted.

"Then why were you lurking around out there like a pair of snoops?"

"We weren't snooping!" Charlie sounded hurt. "We were just too polite to interrupt."

"Anyway," Amelia said quickly. "Lady Naomi sent us – that alien scientist guy was out there in the bush with a scanner he sneaked past you."

Tom looked furious. "Where is he now?"

"He ran off when Lady Naomi tried to bring

47

him here," Charlie said. "She's gone after him."

Tom and Leaf Man exchanged glances.

"What sort of scanner?" asked Leaf Man.

"He's scanning for animals," said Amelia. "He's researching the effect of wormholes on them or something."

"Not looking for the canister then," said Leaf Man. "Whatever's in that thing, it isn't an animal."

"So this guy isn't Guild," said Tom. "He's just some other kind of trouble. That's the closest we've come to a break that I can remember."

"So he's not dangerous then?" Amelia was relieved. She hadn't liked Foxy exactly, but she respected scientific research, and if anyone around here could help her find Grawk, she was willing to give them the benefit of the doubt.

"Dangerous to my career," Tom grumbled. "If Arxish finds out I let an alien illegally transport unregistered tech onto Earth –"

"But not so dangerous you need my help," said Leaf Man, nodding at Tom. "I'm going."

"You're what?" said Tom. "But –"

"Timing is everything," said Leaf Man. "You've seen for yourself how unstable things are getting. How violent and unpredictable the wormholes have become. Doesn't that tell you something?"

"Nothing obvious, no."

"Truly?" Leaf Man tutted. "You've manned this post for decades, Tom. Have you learned nothing in all the years you've sat here and watched?"

"Sat here and watched?" Tom snapped. "*Sat here and watched?* Is that how you see the miserable life I've had? Some old slob just parked on his bum, *watching*? Because I've learned a lot, now that you ask. I've learned that the universe is far bigger than anyone on Earth knows, and that there's not a lot of kindness or fairness out there. I've learned that doing the right thing will cost you more than you can bear, and there will be precious little that comes to you in return for it."

"Oh, Tom."

"Don't pity me!"

"Doesn't someone have to?"

"If you have any pity, then pity Lady Naomi. It's not right that she of all people should have to take responsibility for the blasted thing."

"Which is exactly why I'm going," said Leaf Man, crossing the room and disappearing down the stairs. "To help Lady Naomi. Or at least, since the Nowhere has been stirred up by all this instability, for the first time I've seen a hint of how to find the only person who can."

Amelia glanced at Charlie, who looked just as confused as she was. They were lucky if they ever understood half of what Leaf Man was talking about.

When Leaf Man said nothing more, Tom

grunted, "Get on with it, then." He picked up a length of coiled rope, slung it over his shoulder and began limping towards the door. Then he growled at Amelia and Charlie. "Go on. Get back to your silly party. Leave Lady Naomi and the alien to me. As usual."

He stamped out, leaving Amelia and Charlie standing alone in the cottage.

CHAPTER FIVE

Amelia felt extremely tense walking back towards the hotel. The moon had risen by now, and was lighting their way with a cool silver glow, and far below, at the base of the headland, the sea was beating out its usual soothing music on the cliffs. But all Amelia could think about was Lady Naomi and Tom searching the bush for a rogue scientist, Leaf Man disappearing into the Nowhere on some mysterious quest, Grawk lost and who knew where, and up ahead – worst of all – Sophie T., whom she had abandoned at the hotel without any warning or explanation.

Would she still be there? Amelia wouldn't blame her if she'd called her mum and asked to be picked up.

With a heavy heart, she opened the main doors and stepped into the lobby. Mum was making a phone call at the reception desk, but when she saw Amelia she smiled and pointed to the library.

Amelia braced herself and opened the library door – totally unprepared to find Sophie T. sitting wide-eyed on the sofa, seemingly entranced as James explained one of his gadgets to her.

"It's based on Napier's bones," he was saying, showing her a set. "You see how you can arrange the rods in any order and use them to multiply or divide any numbers with up to nine digits? Well, imagine if instead of using rods to construct a two-dimensional matrix, you used a combination of spheres and cogs to make a three-dimensional system."

Sophie T.'s eyes flicked to the door, saw Amelia, and then flicked straight back to James. "And what would you use it for?"

James hesitated. Amelia knew he couldn't tell Sophie T. he'd been trying to invent a machine to calculate the distortion in the gateway's pattern of wormhole movements. "Err ... it's for – sort of for – that is ..." He looked up and smiled broadly at the sight of his sister. "Amelia! Charlie! Where have you been? Sophie and I have just been, er, waiting for you."

"Yeah, Amelia," Sophie T. said in an ominously sweet voice. "Where have you been?"

Amelia made a face. "I'm so sorry for disappearing on you, Soph, but one of the guests wandered off into the bush and we had to, uh, stop him from getting lost."

Sophie T. looked from Amelia to Charlie, and back to Amelia, uncertain. "Right. So do you often have to run off and rescue random guests?"

"Oh, yeah," said Charlie, so wearily that Amelia almost believed him herself. "Not the Australian ones, of course. *They* know we're not kidding about spiders and snakes and paralyzing ticks and goannas that'll run up your leg and claw your face off. But the overseas ones ... whew. We've got to look out for those guys."

Sophie T., desperate to know whether she was being fooled with, looked to James. He shrugged modestly and nodded. "It's like I told you, Sophie – I didn't know what Amelia and Charlie were up to, but there's always some little emergency that needs to be dealt with straightaway."

Amelia saw Sophie T.'s shoulders hitch up towards her ears, and her fingers curl into the fabric of her skirt. She was staring at James, waiting for some signal in his face of whether he was telling her the truth.

James gazed back, unruffled, and then Sophie T. smiled and let out a deep breath. "Of course. I knew it was something like that."

"Well." James got to his feet. "Nice talking to you, Sophie. I'll tell Mum you're ready for that movie now, Amelia."

"Thank you," she said, meaning more than just the movie.

"What are we going to see?" Sophie T. asked, eagerly taking up the change in subject. "Is it on DVD or Blu-ray? Oh – do you have a 3-D TV?"

"Actually," Amelia said, "we don't have a TV at all."

"Really? Oh." Sophie T. was unperturbed. "So you just watch everything on your laptops?"

Charlie laughed. "They don't have any computers either."

Sophie T. narrowed her eyes. Despite deciding to accept their excuse for running off on her, she was clearly still worried that they were laughing at her somehow. "OK then, smarty, so how are we supposed to watch a movie?"

"On that," said Amelia, pointing to the old reel-to-reel film projector that was sitting on its cart beside the rolled-up projection screen.

Sophie T. blinked. "And what movie are we going to watch on *that*?"

"Um ..." Amelia gulped and hoped very hard that Dad had gotten something good. "I'm not sure, let me check."

She slipped out to the lobby and saw that Mum was on her way with a large, thick plastic disk tucked under her arm: the can of film.

"What is it?" Amelia asked.

Mum grinned. "Have a look for yourself." She held the can out to Amelia. It was heavier than Amelia expected and had a paper label stuck to it, with untidy handwriting telling her the title was ...

"*Spring Kisses*?" Amelia was puzzled. "But ..."

"What?!" Sophie T. yelped from inside the library. "What did you say?"

Amelia showed her the can.

"*Spring Kisses*?" Sophie T. gasped, then shrieked. "The actual, genuine *Spring Kisses* with Harry Badenburger?"

"Yes, I think so," said Mum. "Was that a good choice?"

Sophie T. grabbed the film from Amelia's hands and hugged it to her chest, jumping up and down with such feverish joy Charlie took a step back.

"This is unbelievable!" she cried. "This movie isn't even out in theaters for another month – how did you get it? It's impossible!"

Mum and Amelia looked at each other. How could they explain why a little family in a crumbling hotel in a nowhere town on the edge of Australia had a copy of the biggest teen movie in the last fifteen years that *no one* had even been able to *preview*? Imagine if – after all their problems with cyborg rats, Guild mercenaries, and ancient starships – their cover ended up being blown by Sophie T.'s knowledge of movie release dates!

Sophie T., though, was too excited to let the oddness of the situation waste a single second of her time. "Can we put it on now?" she pleaded. "Right now?"

"Of course!" Mum said brightly, thrilled to avoid explaining her way around Control's connections with the movie industry.

Charlie, meanwhile, shot daggers at Amelia.

"What?" she said.

"*Spring Kisses?*" he said with distaste. "Are you for real?"

Amelia shrugged. "My dad was in charge of what we got."

Charlie snorted. "What happened to getting

59

Ninja Cops on Mars?"

"Yeah, that was *your* choice, Charlie, not mine."

"But you can't really want to see this film," he said kindly. "I mean, I get that Sophie T. does, but not you, Amelia."

"Why not me?"

"Because ... because ..." he spluttered.

"Is there a problem?" said Mum, threading the film through the projector's spools, while Sophie T. set up the screen.

"No, not at all," Amelia said, sitting on the sofa. "Charlie just figured out I'm a girl."

"Oh," Sophie T. smirked. "*Boys*."

Charlie didn't reply, but sat down on the other side of Amelia with an air of heroic resignation.

"Oops, quick!" said Dad from behind them, just as Mum flicked on the projector and Sophie T. sat on Amelia's other side. There was a soft purr from the old motor, and a square of light appeared on the screen, flickering before it was replaced by an honest-to-goodness old-fashioned countdown.

"Before it begins," said Dad, "I've got a whole dinner in forty-five-degree sectors for you!"

He set down two big plates of food: one of pizza slices, and the other of watermelon.

Looking much more cheerful now that there was food in the room, Charlie helped himself to pizza and settled down to endure the movie. Sophie T. squeezed Amelia's arm and whispered, "Sophie F. and Shani will *die* when they find out what they missed!" Amelia settled into the sofa cushions, smiling.

It turned out that the movie was pretty dull. Harry Badenburger was so gorgeous it wasn't funny, but the movie wasn't funny either, and Amelia was almost sure it was supposed to be. Even Sophie T. had to admit that he didn't make a very convincing international diamond thief. When the sad and lonely (but totally beautiful and rich) main girl confronted Harry at the top of the Eiffel Tower, saying, "You're nothing but a common thief – I know you stole my necklace," and he replied, "All's fair in love and war. After all, you stole my *heart*," all three kids covered their faces with their hands and howled.

"No wonder nobody's leaked the film on the Internet yet," said Sophie T. "Who could be bothered?"

Amelia giggled. "I don't know, I think it's starting to grow on me. Look – Harry's about to burst into song again."

Sophie T. rolled her eyes and turned away from the screen in contempt. She lolled on the arm of the sofa and made a gagging noise, which made Charlie laugh, and then jerked upright with such violence she knocked the pizza out of Amelia's hands. As Harry Badenburger hit a high C, Sophie T. went a whole octave better and *screamed*.

"It's bad," Charlie agreed. "But not *that* bad."

"It's a ghost!" Sophie T.'s voice was so constricted by fear, little more than a gasp came out. "Look – a vampire!"

She pointed and Amelia saw something glowing yellow outside the library's French doors. Two somethings, seeming to hover about three feet from the ground. Almost like ghostly eyes, staring straight at them. Amelia's heart sped up in recognition, but then she caught herself. No, it couldn't be Grawk out there. But if not, then ... *what*?

Sophie T. wasn't stopping to wonder. Before Amelia could say anything, she was already out the library door and across the lobby. Amelia and Charlie rushed to follow.

The lobby was quiet at this time of night, but Mum was standing over at the reception desk, busy with a couple of guests. Amelia did a double take: no, that wasn't a guest. It was Lady Naomi, and she was holding Foxy firmly by the elbow (though he was, of course, holo-disguised once more as the man in the corduroy suit).

"I'm trying to tell you, my research is time sensitive!" Foxy was whining. "If I'd waited for approval, I'd have missed the whole reason for the study."

"Mmm, very frustrating," Mum agreed. "But not my concern."

"How can you say that? How is it *not your concern* to see science and exploration push back the darkness of ignorance? How is it –"

Mum regarded him levelly. "You can save your breath, sir. My concern is to see that every one of the people in this hotel is safe."

"But science –"

"Is extremely important. But people matter

more. I'm keeping this." She took the bio-scanner off the desk in front of her, put it into the hotel's safe, and locked it without further comment.

Sophie T. took that as her cue and dashed over to Mum and Lady Naomi without a single glance at the fuming man with them.

"Mrs. Walker! Mrs. Walker! Excuse me, but –"

Mum shot a glance at Amelia who tried to shrug (*I couldn't help it*) and grimace (*sorry!*) and look serious (*but there* is *a problem*) all at the same time.

Mum seemed confused, but nodded her head towards the man (*OK, Amelia, but you can see I'm busy*) before saying to Sophie T., "I'm so sorry, dear, but I have to finish my work here before I can talk with you." She lifted her eyebrows at Amelia. "Perhaps Scott or Mary could help you? Or James is somewhere."

Sophie T. blushed in embarrassment and said calmly, "I'm sorry to interrupt you, Mrs. Walker."

"That's perfectly all right." Mum smiled at her warmly, but quickly turned back to Lady Naomi and Foxy.

Sophie T. turned away just as quickly, looking dangerously close to tears, and whispered, "That was so humiliating."

"No, it was fine," Amelia assured her. "Come on – Mum's right. Let's go and find Dad. He's probably in the kitchen and we can at least get some cake for a midnight feast."

Sophie T. shook her head. "No, don't. I was just imagining things. I can't even remember now what I thought I saw."

"You said it was a ghost," Charlie reminded her. "Or a vampire. You didn't decide."

"Yes, thank you, Charles. Like I said: I was just using my imagination. Obviously it was just a possum in the bushes."

"Except there *aren't* any bushes outsi–"

"Yeah, thank you, Charlie!" Amelia kicked him in the ankle. "Anyway, who's tired?"

"What?" Charlie rubbed his ankle.

Sophie T. was quicker on the uptake. "I don't know if I'm ready to sleep yet, but I can't wait to see your room."

CHAPTER SIX

Sophie T. instantly approved of Amelia's four-poster bed and the deep bay window that jutted out like her own private observation deck, giving a view of nearly the whole headland.

"This is like a fairy-tale room!" she sighed. "You're like Rapunzel or something."

"Except her mum isn't an evil witch," Charlie pointed out.

Sophie T. ignored him and instead pointed to Amelia's single bed, which Dad had brought out of the storeroom and put by the wall. "Is that where I'm sleeping?"

"Oh," Amelia said. "No. I mean, unless you'd prefer to? But there's so much room in the four-poster, I thought you could share it with me. Charlie was going to sleep in that one."

"Charlie's sleeping in the same room as we are?"

"Well ... yeah. I mean, it's a big room, and there are curtains around the bed, if you're ..."

"No, it's fine," said Sophie T. "I've just never shared a room with a *boy* before."

"What's wrong with boys?" Charlie asked.

Sophie T. looked at him sideways. "Where would I begin, Charles?"

"How about with how awesome we are? Or how tough? Or how we're never afraid of the dark?"

Sophie T. sucked in a breath, and then returned, "Or how silly you are? Or how smelly and ugly and *hairy*?"

Charlie hooted. "You don't think that about

Barry Hamburger. You think he's *gorgeous*."

"Well, he is. Plus he's totally talented –"

Charlie hooted again.

"– and he writes his own music."

"And," Charlie added, grinning triumphantly, "is a boy."

"He's not a boy, Charles. *You're* a boy. Harry Badenburger is a *guy*."

"What's the difference?"

"I'll tell you ..."

"Guys," Amelia said quietly. Then, "Guys?"

"Go on," Charlie said stubbornly. "Tell me what?"

"Guys!"

"There's hardly any point." Sophie T. crossed her arms. "Seeing as you're too thick to understand."

"*Guys!*" Amelia raised her voice and the two of them looked at her, guilty, and then at each other, accusing.

"I'm very sorry, Amelia," Sophie T. said, still glaring at Charlie. "I'll just go brush my teeth and get changed in the bathroom. Where it's *private*."

She got her overnight bag and strode past Charlie, her nose in the air.

Amelia sighed.

"I'm sorry," said Charlie when she was gone.

"Yeah, sure."

"I am! But also, I was only trying to do you a favor."

Amelia rolled her eyes at him.

"It's true! I'll bet you anything Sophie T. has completely forgotten about what happened downstairs."

"Hey!" Amelia hurried to stand right beside him and whispered, "What do you think it was?"

"For a moment, I thought it had to be Grawk."

"Me too!"

"But then, how?" Charlie asked. "Grawk on a

71

ladder? Wearing magnifying spectacles?"

"Yeah," Amelia deflated.

"Anyway," he went on. "Whatever it was, there's no way we can find out with Sophie T. around."

"I know." Amelia gazed sadly at her window.

It took ages to fall asleep. First they had to all get ready to turn off the light, then they talked, then Sophie T. told Charlie to tell Amelia about the time Ms. Slaviero brought an orphaned fruit bat to school and it got spooked by the bell and flew onto Dean's head and hung on to his face so tightly that no one could peel it off again.

Then finally there was nothing more to say, and Amelia stopped thinking about Sophie T. and strange yellow glows and Grawk and Foxy and Lady Naomi and mysterious canisters, and instead just lay quietly, enjoying how cozy it was to be snuggled in bed ...

And then, right next to her ear, a little explosion of warm breath went, "*Psssst!*"

Amelia bolted awake. "Who's there?"

"Shh!"

"Charlie?" Amelia sat up straighter. He was crouched on the floor beside her. "What's going on?"

"Listen!"

Amelia frowned into the darkness and waited. After a moment, she heard a scraping noise on the roof. Not the scuffling, wrestling noises in the ceiling that rats made; this was heavier, but also quieter, more distant. And it was undoubtedly *outside*. Something was walking on the hotel, and every now and then a tile shifted under its feet.

"I hear it," she said. "But what –" She froze as an almost familiar growl rumbled above her. "Could it be Grawk?"

"Something's happened to him, if it is," said

Charlie.

"Well, I have to find out." Amelia wriggled out of bed, then listened to the steady breathing beside her. As far as she could tell, Sophie T. was still asleep. "Come on," she whispered. "Find your shoes."

"I don't know," Charlie whispered back, but she could hear him feeling around on the floor. "You don't know it was Grawk. Or maybe it was *a* grawk, but not your nice Grawk. What if another wild grawk came though? Or something else?"

"Something else that sounds like Grawk?"

"Or something that knows how to sound like what you most want to hear. To lure you out, like bait."

Overhead, there was a heavy clattering, a deep, malevolent growl, and then a shadow flickered past the starry sky outside Amelia's window. Whatever the thing was, it had just leapt off the roof to the grass two stories below. Amelia pushed past Charlie and ran to the window. There was enough moonlight to make out a streak of movement on the lawn below.

"It's Grawk," she whispered joyfully.

"How can you –"

"It *was*. And he's going to Tom's. Let's go!"

"Amelia," Charlie hissed, but she was already slipping out of her bedroom door. He followed her across the gallery, down the marble stairs, and into the lobby. "Amelia, think about it. You don't know for sure that was Grawk."

"I do. I know his growl."

"Right – his growl," said Charlie. "That wasn't exactly a happy noise, was it?"

Amelia let herself out the main doors of the hotel, and sat down on the top step to put her shoes on.

"Even if it is Grawk," Charlie went on, sitting

beside her with his shoes, "and it probably was, OK? But even then – why do you think it's a good idea to chase him in the dark? What if he wants us to leave him alone?"

"Then why was he watching us in the library? Why was he on the roof above my bedroom?"

"For all I know, he was looking for a chimney to come down, and we were going to be the three little pigs inside."

"No." Amelia wasn't about to waste time arguing. "It was Grawk, and he was helping us. I don't know if he was standing guard over us or trying to get our attention to show us something, but I'm going to find him."

"Amelia –"

She'd taken long enough already. Shoes on, she ran into the dark and called back, "Stay here or come with me, I don't care, but I'm going."

Charlie ran after her. "Of course I'm coming."

They sped through the grass, down the steep slope towards the magnolia grove. Amelia took a deep breath as they entered the thicker darkness under the trees. They couldn't run here but had to pick their way through the leaf litter, feeling ahead for low-hanging branches. They were still under cover when, across the clearing ahead of them, they saw of a flash of white light coming from the other side of Tom's cottage. Amelia and Charlie stopped and listened. Another flash. And then two more, and the sound of voices, a way off through the trees beyond Tom's.

Amelia saw a faint yellow glow in the bushes off to one side, a distance from where the voices seemed to be.

"Grawk!" she called softly – the yellow globes blinked twice and then vanished.

Charlie shoved her. "Look!" he pointed.

While Amelia had been looking at the glow,

that flashing light had come towards them. She heard footsteps treading through dry leaves, saw branches shiver as they were shoved aside and then an enormous creature stepped into the clearing, its attention focused on the gadget in its hands.

It was easily the muscliest being Amelia had ever seen, and not just in real life: even including Charlie's superhero comics. Grotesque ropey veins covered bulging arms, and vast shoulders rose to a smallish head, which was completely covered by a spiked metal helmet. The gadget lit up again, bathing the alien in an intense light. Amelia saw dull, slate-blue skin covered with intricate patterns that looked halfway between tattoos and scars. The creature grunted, shook the gadget and called back over its shoulder. Its voice was like a nightmare version of Dad grinding beans in his coffee machine.

A second blue giant stepped into the clearing. This one was bigger still, with no spikes on its helmet but a wild beard springing out from underneath instead. And if that wasn't horrible enough, it was dragging little Foxy in his centaur form behind it by one spindly arm.

Charlie sucked in a breath and they both crouched lower behind the trees.

Foxy yipped at them, his attempts to speak their grumbling language sounding thin and frightened, but – Amelia noticed – still cranky. He held his head high, and he yanked his arm out of Beard's grip. Spike growled something and shoved the gadget at him. Foxy took it, inspected its workings, and then the giant tapped it forcefully and growled again.

It's broken, Amelia guessed. And why wouldn't it be, with that massive blue finger thumping it like a hammer blow?

Foxy yipped sharply and pulled the gadget back out of Spike's reach. He pressed something and light glowed up into his face. Amelia saw him frown as he adjusted its controls.

Then there was another great burst of light, and Amelia realized it was blasting out in a thin sheet, scanning the bush from top to bottom in a ninety-degree spread. The edge of this light was only three or four feet from her hiding spot with Charlie, and the two kids held their breath.

Foxy, still looking at the box, gave a yip of surprise and in a jumble of excited growls, pointed into the patch of bush. The two blue giants immediately tapped their helmets so that visors dropped down over their eyes (*night vision?* Amelia wondered), and turned to follow Foxy's finger. They were wearing backpacks with weapons strapped to the side, and more holstered on their thighs. These guys weren't messing around.

Amelia squeezed Charlie's arm. That yellow glow that she so deeply hoped and believed was Grawk had vanished into the very area Beard was now aiming his gun.

Foxy yipped and growled again, and then all three aliens suddenly ran, the bio-scanner flaring out again as they smashed their way through the bush.

"What was that about?" Charlie breathed as soon as the clearing was empty.

The aliens were making so much noise that he and Amelia didn't need to worry about being overheard, but both of them felt safer whispering. Amelia hoped wherever Grawk was, he was too fast and too clever to be in danger.

"That scanner ..." said Amelia. "They have to be tracking something, right?" She tried not to think about what could possibly be out here that would take that many weapons to bring down.

"Or some*one*," said Charlie. He glanced back the way the giant creatures had come. "They were really close to the cottage. They probably just came out of the gateway."

"Which means –"

They both darted towards the cottage. "Tom!"

Sprinting across the clearing, Amelia saw that Tom's door was ajar. A weak light spilled out over the front step, and it was so *quiet* inside that Amelia knew nothing good could have happened.

She and Charlie hesitated for a moment, but with the aliens out there in the bush (not to mention whatever they were tracking), it surely couldn't be more dangerous for them in here?

Charlie swallowed hard and pushed the door open. Amelia followed him in. Tom's place was a disaster. It was always messy, but usually the mess had some kind of order. This was the chaos of a house that had been ransacked. Boxes had been thrown across the room, their contents scattered. The charts James had carefully organized were strewn over the floor, and Tom's lamp – the only source of light right now – had been knocked over.

"But where's Tom?" said Amelia.

"He's here," said Charlie, looking around the door into the gateway room. Tom lay flat on his back, his eye wide-open, unmoving.

CHAPTER SEVEN

Charlie squatted down and patted Tom's cheek. When nothing happened, he put his ear to Tom's chest to check if his heart was still beating, and a finger under Tom's nose to feel for his breath.

"Unconscious," he said. "Totally out of it, but otherwise fine, I reckon." Without warning, he peeked under Tom's eye patch.

"Charlie!"

"What? As if you've never been curious."

"Not *that* curious."

Amelia brought over an old crocheted blanket

from the back of the sofa and Charlie tried to roll Tom over onto his side. Tom, though, was completely rigid.

"It's almost like ..." Charlie said, grunting with the effort, and then giving up suddenly. Tom rocked on the floor as though he were a statue, not an actual person. "... like he's been petrified."

Amelia winced at the thought, and spread the blanket over him – a useless gesture if he *had* been turned to stone, but she had to do something. They returned to the front room, searching for the box James had put all of Foxy's confiscated property into. Amelia was utterly unsurprised to see it lying empty on the floor behind Tom's desk. Whatever Foxy and his giant friends had come to do, they were now fully equipped.

Amelia picked up Tom's phone and saw that the spiraling cord that connected the old-fashioned handset to the dialing part had been cut.

"Look." She showed Charlie the severed wires. "We've got to tell Mum and Dad."

With one last look back at Tom, Amelia and Charlie raced out of the cottage and back through the trees. They were right at the foot of the headland, looking up the steep slope to the hotel, when the moon came out from behind a haze of cloud, casting a clear light over everything. Charlie was about to run out onto the open grass, but Amelia grabbed his arm – she'd spotted the three aliens bursting out of the bush beyond the hedge maze.

There was a blast of light from the scanner in Foxy's hands, and then a piercing scream from a completely different direction.

"Oh, no," said Charlie.

"Sophie T.!" Amelia was horrified to see her friend standing on the brow of the hill – just where the rest of them had stood earlier to watch the fireworks. "What's she doing there?"

"*Not* being left out."

"What about her being afraid of the dark?"

"Apparently she would literally rather die than be left behind."

"Don't say that!" Amelia moved out of the grove. "We've got to help her."

This time it was Charlie who held Amelia back. "Yeah, but not by being caught."

Amelia watched as all three aliens began running towards Sophie T. Her own heart was racing – she couldn't imagine how Sophie T.'s must be. "OK, we don't get caught," she agreed. "But then what?"

The two blue giants were barreling up the slope like charging elephants, running shoulder to shoulder, and then suddenly they split apart: one circling out to the right, the other to the left, so that as they drew closer to Sophie T., they were also cutting off her escape back to the hotel.

"They're rounding her up like sheepdogs," hissed Charlie. "Enormous rhino sheepdogs."

"Charlie, what are we going to do?"

"And here comes Foxy ..."

Foxy was nowhere near as quick as the giants, but he was direct. Instead of helping the giants outflank Sophie T., he ran straight at her, yipping and growling the whole time.

"Tom's out cold, Leaf Man's in the Nowhere," Amelia thought out loud. "Mum and Dad are in the hotel. So's Lady Naomi probably, but we can't get there without going past *them* –"

As Foxy drew closer to Sophie T., she began to shrink back from him.

Charlie groaned. "Look behind you, Sophie, you dope. Haven't you ever watched a horror movie?"

By stumbling *away* from Foxy, Sophie T. was walking straight into the waiting hands of Spike and Beard.

Foxy yipped and waved a hand (Amelia thought he was telling off the giants, warning them to leave Sophie T. alone), but it only made Sophie T. back away faster. Finally realizing that his natural form and voice were making things worse, Foxy switched on his holo-emitter.

The shabby corduroy man appeared and began speaking to Sophie T. in English. His high voice carried clearly in the still night air, and Amelia could hear that it was shaking. Foxy must be freaking out, too. "It's OK," he quavered. "Nothing's going to happen. You're OK."

Beard growled. "In English," snapped Foxy. "The poor child is frightened enough as it is."

Beard snorted, then rasped, "You think we care if it's frightened? Get rid of it. We've got less than an hour before our wormhole leaves, and so far you've achieved nothing."

At the sound of a new voice behind her, Sophie

T. spun on the spot and reeled back as she took in the enormous creature towering over her. She gave a cry – not so much a scream as a choking in-breath of dismay – and then Spike pointed at her, a light flashed, and ... nothing. Sophie T. didn't move. She didn't so much as squeak, or even drop the hand that was lifted partway to her mouth. It was as though she'd been frozen, or ...

"Petrified," whispered Charlie.

"At least we've caught something," said Spike. "It's only a tiny little wriggler, but better than nothing."

"We're not taking a human child!" Foxy yipped. "This has nothing to do with the contract I signed."

"Contract?" sneered Beard. "Do you see any contract lawyers around? We're here to turn a profit, and if you've got any brains in that tiny head of yours, you'll do what we tell you. And quickly."

Foxy, to his credit, did not back down. Hands on hips, he said, "I'm a scientist, not some hired thug. This is a little *girl* – native to this planet. I agreed to help return a feral animal to its home planet, *not* kidnap a person from hers. Profit has nothing to do with my motives."

Beard began to tremble and heave, his breathing becoming jerky, noisy and more horrible than anything Amelia had heard so far. She realized he was laughing. "Pick it up," he said to Spike. "We'll deal with our little *scientist* later, once the mission is completed."

Spike picked up Sophie T., tucked her under his arm like an umbrella, and laughed in Foxy's face.

"How much less frightened is she, now that she's heard all that in English?" he guffawed, and then turned and followed Beard into the bush.

Foxy stood uselessly for a heartbeat or two in the moonlight, and then scurried after them.

CHAPTER EIGHT

Amelia, still crouched and hiding, covered her face in her hands. "Oh no. Oh, we're dead. Sophie T.'s dead!"

"Not yet," said Charlie. "It doesn't sound like they're going to eat her, so that's good."

"Yeah, but –" Amelia took a deep breath, trying to get some sense into herself. "But what do we do? We can't stop them. No one in Forgotten Bay would be strong enough to get in their way."

"Tom has that shotgun."

"And Tom's unconscious – same as Sophie T.,

I'm guessing – *and* his place is in the opposite direction to those guys."

"Who are totally getting away while we talk about it," Charlie pointed out, helpful as ever.

"What about Mum and Dad? And James? Have they seriously just *slept* through all of that?"

"Look," said Charlie. "Hotel: that way." He pointed up the hill to their right. "Kidnapping space giants and Sophie T.: that way." He pointed down to the bush ahead of them, and to the left. "And they're moving fast. Choose."

"I could –"

"No," he cut her off. "We don't split up. I don't mind doing something insanely dangerous, even if it is only Sophie T. we're trying to save, but I won't do it alone."

"But I was –"

"And neither will you."

Amelia groaned in frustration. He was right,

and she knew it, so their only options were raising the alarm (by which time, who would know where they had taken Sophie T.?) or ...

"There's no choice." Amelia got to her feet. "We have to go after them, and –"

"Yeah?"

"Hope for an opportunity," she finished lamely. "I think the best we can do is try to catch up."

"Good enough," said Charlie. "Let's go."

Even without a plan, it was good to be moving. Just the physical work of running uphill, thinking where the aliens could be headed, and listening for clues, cleared Amelia's mind. She was too busy to feel the full force of her fear, and to worry about what might happen next. All she had to do was find the trail.

They reached the edge of the lawn beyond the hedge maze, and paused in front of the wall of dense bush.

"Which way?" said Charlie.

Amelia scanned left and right, wondering if the aliens had actually been headed anywhere, or if they were just randomly plowing through the trees.

"Wouldn't you think guys that big would leave a more obvious path?" said Charlie.

"Maybe if we could see as well as Lady Naomi –" Something caught Amelia's eye: the faintest suggestion of a yellow glow amongst the undergrowth, and then it was gone. "That way, come on!"

The bush was vicious. Serrated leaves and thorny twigs grabbed at them with every step, and their pajamas were not designed to cope with any of it. "I'm sleeping in jeans from now on," puffed Charlie.

"Look, look!"

Ahead, a good-sized branch of a banksia tree

was snapped in half and dangling. It was so high up that Amelia could only have touched the break with the tips of her fingers at a full stretch.

"They're making a path through – yeah, see? There." She pointed in the darkness. "The ferns have all been squashed flat."

They picked up speed, then slowed down again almost immediately. They wanted to follow the aliens, not catch up to them. Through a gully, then a grove of straggly trees (more branches snapped), and up a rocky rise, and then so deep into the bush they were far past the farthest they'd ever been. And that had been with Lady Naomi and in full daylight. And then they saw the aliens.

But where was Sophie T.?

Several small trees had been knocked down and piled to one side, making a rough clearing. The giants had taken off their backpacks and Spike was rummaging through his.

Amelia and Charlie hunched down behind a boulder and watched. Foxy was still engrossed in his scanner. Beard was noisily chewing on something, and scratching his belly contentedly. Charlie nudged Amelia: there was Sophie T., still in that exact position they'd last seen her, with a hand partially raised. Only she wasn't standing now, she'd been laid down on the ground, and was almost hidden in the long grass. Safe – for now.

Spike stood up straight, yawned, and began humming as he fussed with his backpack, hardly paying any attention to Sophie T.

They don't seem interested in her at all, Amelia thought. *Then what? What could get these giants to team up with Foxy?*

Spike laughed and then said to Foxy, "So where's the beast? You said you had a signal."

"I have," Foxy yipped. "Or I did. These animals are incredibly hard to track."

"No more excuses!" snapped Beard. "If we miss the wormhole, we miss the sale, and if that happens, I think you'll find it *incredibly hard* to make it up to us."

"Sale?" said Foxy. "What sale?"

Beard snorted. "You don't think we came all the way out to Earth without having a buyer lined up already, did you?"

"But I never agreed to help you *sell* a wild animal – I was helping you save it!"

"Oh, you're helping, all right," said Spike. "Helping save our business. Helping our reputations –"

"Helping us make a good impression on the Guild," Beard added.

Charlie nudged Amelia again, and she saw what he'd noticed: Sophie T.'s fingers were beginning to twitch. Whatever Spike had done to petrify her, it was starting to wear off. But how long before Sophie T. could move enough to get away? The moon was so bright, Charlie and Amelia had no chance of sneaking over and carrying her off without being caught too.

Amelia turned to look back the way they'd come. *How long would it take us to go get Mum and Dad?* And then she realized something terrible. *I don't remember the way home – I think we're lost.*

They were as trapped as Sophie T., with no way to get help. Even if they somehow stole Sophie T. back from the aliens, what could they do next? There was nowhere safe for them to go, and nowhere to hide as long as Foxy had that scanner. Unless Charlie knew how to get back to the hotel ...

She turned to ask Charlie, but found to her horror that he was gone. A moment later, she spotted his pale face on the other side of the clearing, peeking out from behind the pile of ripped up trees. Her whole body was flooded with relief, but then she froze: *If I can see him, then he can see me. And if we can see each other, then what if –*

Before she could finish her thought, a hand the size of a garbage-can lid had snatched her from behind the rock. Charlie blurred out of view, but she could still *hear* him clearly enough. "Oh, no you don't!" he yelled. "You put me down!"

The alien did – and a second later, Amelia was plonked into the grass too, right next to him and Sophie T.

"Nice work," grinned Beard. "Three human pups will bring an excellent price."

Amelia shuffled over to Sophie T. and put an arm around her. She was as stiff as a doll, but her hand was now clenched into a fist. The grass rustled around them.

"Do you think our buyer will be interested?"

Beard scoffed. "The pit mistress won't be interested in them!"

"Pit mistress?" said Foxy. "You don't mean – are you telling me you intend to sell that magnificent grawk to a pit-fighting gang?"

Amelia looked at Charlie, horrified. They were hunting Grawk!

Charlie nodded grimly, but then shot Amelia a significant look. Her eyes widened as she guessed what he was thinking: things were looking very bad for them – almost Krskn-level bad, with all this talk of being sold to aliens – but they'd just heard a chink opening in the aliens' plan.

"You savages!" Foxy howled. "I thought you were selling to a zoo, at least – but pit fighting? You butchers!"

Yep. Foxy was no longer on the space giants' side. That left the tiniest hope he might decide to be on theirs.

"Try to move," Charlie whispered to Sophie T. "If you can hear me, if you're not still unconscious, try to move. We're going to try to rescue you."

Sophie T. lay frozen, not even an eyelid flickered, but she made a little grunt in the back of her throat that sounded a lot like, "Huh!" Amelia noticed her fist tightening until the knuckles bulged.

"She can hear us," she said, and began massaging Sophie T.'s hand and wrist. "She's trying."

"Oh, I am sick of your yapping," Beard growled, and Amelia started, thinking he was speaking to her. But the giant was still staring down at Foxy. "You took the job, now *do* the job. I doubt you'll have anything to complain about when you get paid."

Amelia sank lower into the grass.

"It's working," Charlie breathed as Sophie T.'s shoulders moved under his clumsy back rub.

"It's not about the money!" Foxy said. "I wanted to save –"

"Look," Spike sighed. "It's only one grawk. Look at the big picture: are you going to save it, or save yourself? Because only one of you is going to come out of this happy. Why not you?"

Foxy turned away, muttering furiously.

"Just get on with it," Beard shouted.

Sophie T., meanwhile, was now beginning to wiggle both feet, and her face was slowly melting to form a new expression. It was an expression of pure terror, but even that looked better to Amelia than the awful stiff blank her face had been before.

Foxy yelped with alarm, and for a second Amelia thought he'd spotted Sophie T.'s gradual recovery. But he was staring at his scanner in amazement. "It's here!" he yipped. "The grawk. It's –"

"Where?" said Beard. "I don't see anything."

"You won't – oh." Foxy shook the scanner and

knocked it with the heel of his hand. "There's something wrong with it – this doesn't make sense – it's not –"

"Stop gibbering!" Beard bellowed. "It's not what?"

"Not possible!" Foxy gasped. "Never heard of –"

"What?" said Spike. "*What?*"

Foxy only pointed into the bush, his face as contorted with fear as Sophie T.'s. The two alien giants and three human children all looked.

At first there was nothing but the tangled black wall of the surrounding bush. No sound, no movement, not the slightest shiver of a clue of what was to come. And then two yellow saucers glowed through the undergrowth and a deep grinding noise rang out in the night air, filling Amelia with terrified joy as Grawk sprang into the clearing – as huge and solid and ferocious as a tiger.

CHAPTER NINE

It was Grawk all right, but a Grawk of nightmare proportions. His face was split into a vicious snarl, his sharp white teeth all bared and his eyes narrowed down to yellow slits. His head was lowered over his paws, and his broad black shoulders were braced and ready to pounce.

Foxy gazed at him with a kind of wondering fear, but Beard and Spike didn't even blink – they drew their weapons from their thigh holsters and took aim.

"Ready?" said Beard.

"No!" Amelia scrambled to her feet and ran to stand between him and Grawk. It was only when she saw the barrel of his gun pointed at *her* that she realized what she'd done, but there was no backing down now. "Don't hurt him, *please*."

Behind her, Grawk's growl rose again, and all the hair on the back of her neck stood up. She wasn't completely sure whether the biggest danger was the gun in front of her, or all those teeth behind her.

"We're not going to hurt it," said Beard. "That's a pretty little fortune right there. *You*, on the other hand, are totally expendable, so you might want to get out of the way."

"Or not," said Spike, and he shot Grawk from his angle instead.

A beam of plasma knocked Grawk to the ground, and Amelia spun around to see him lying stiff. *No!*

Beard walked over to Grawk, casually shoving Amelia aside, and shot him again. This weapon blasted an explosive net over the helpless animal, and as Amelia watched, thick fibers wrapped around him and began to shrink tight. In only moments, he was wrapped up like a package.

"Right," said Beard, turning to Foxy. "Now that we've got our grawk, no thanks to you, maybe you'd like to explain why it's ten times bigger than you said."

Foxy was now so excited, he seemed to have forgotten their argument. He trotted over to Grawk and scanned him again. Amelia stubbornly crept back to stand as close to Grawk as she could. The aliens ignored her.

"Yes, look – I'm right," Foxy said. "He's only six to eight months old. He isn't due for his first growth spurt until his birthday, but – oh!" He stepped closer again, almost dancing in his delight. "This is exactly what all my studies predicted!"

Beard growled, "Then why didn't you predict it for us?"

Foxy waved away the comment. "I couldn't foresee the specific results, but you take a creature from its home planet, expose it to different gravity, let it breathe a different atmosphere, sit under a different sun, eat totally different food – well, of course, ninety-five percent of creatures in that situation will simply die. But that other five percent, oh my!"

"Whoa," Charlie hissed to Amelia. "Grawk is Superman!"

"This is great," said Spike. "Way beyond the buyer's expectations. We're going to have to increase the price."

"If it's that simple," said Foxy, backing away from Grawk.

"Money is always that simple," Beard chuckled.

"Yes, but biology isn't. How much did you blast him with?" Foxy's eyes flickered towards Grawk. Amelia followed his gaze, and her breath caught in her throat.

"A single shot. Fifteen hundred centigrams," said Spike. "Why?"

Foxy scrabbled backward, his eyes wide with shock. "Because he's already coming out of it. Watch out!"

"Relax," said Beard – but he took a nervous step back all the same. "The netting will –"

He was silenced by an almighty shredding sound as Grawk heaved himself to his feet, flexing his shoulders, tearing the netting to tatters. Amelia was close enough to feel some of the fibers rain down on her head, but nobody else was paying any attention to her. Not even Grawk – his attention was fixed on Beard, with one ear cocked towards Spike.

Amelia took the opportunity to scurry back to Charlie and Sophie T., who was sitting up now and trembling all over – whether from fear alone, or the aftereffects of that petrifying shot, Amelia couldn't tell. Either way, she didn't look up to any quick escapes through the bush just yet.

"Not Superman," said Charlie. "Grawk is the Hulk! And they've just made him mad."

"What if you're right?" Amelia asked. "What if Grawk *is* like the Hulk, and he's too angry to remember who he is? Who we are?"

"Well, he knows who the bad guys are, anyway," said Charlie as Grawk lashed his tail and paced towards Beard.

Beard didn't move; he kept his eyes locked with Grawk's, but he growled to Spike.

Spike growled back, and dialed his plasma gun up until its tip glowed. He raised it, sighted along the barrel and took aim.

"Run, Grawk!" Amelia screamed.

Spike shot. This time the plasma was a burning streak through the darkness, but Grawk was gone by the time it reached its mark.

Beard roared in frustration, and Spike swung his gun towards the patch of bush Grawk had leapt to, but he had utterly vanished.

"You did it!" Charlie cheered. "He listened to you – it's still Grawk!"

"You did it," snarled Beard, snatching Amelia up and holding her in the air by the scruff of the neck like a puppy. "So now you can be the bait in our trap. The beast obviously responds to you."

"He doesn't," Amelia choked out, no idea if she was telling the truth or not. She clawed at Beard's hand, trying to wriggle out of his grip. "He's forgotten me and gone feral. He just got scared when I yelled."

"Scared?" said Spike. "*That* thing?"

"Why don't we do a little experiment and find out?" Beard grinned. "Call him back for us, there's a good human."

Amelia's faced turned purple as Beard squeezed her, but she wheezed, "No. I won't help you."

"Not even to save your own life?" he asked, almost politely.

That was a horrible thought, but Amelia knew he'd rather be able to sell her as a slave if he couldn't catch Grawk. That wasn't exactly comforting, but it meant he was bluffing about killing her.

"I don't betray my friends," she panted.

"Right. Thanks for the tip."

Amelia gasped for breath as Beard's grip on her shifted, and for a second the world swam groggily around her. Just when she thought he was going to turn her upside down, she realized he'd stooped to pick something up. He brought his hands in front of him so Amelia could see what it was. It was Sophie T.

"Here's the deal," said Beard. "Keep protecting the grawk, and I'll do something very mean and unnecessary to your friend here." He shook Sophie T. to underline his point. "*Or*," he grinned smugly, "save your fellow human and give up the feral animal you said yourself has forgotten you."

It was an impossible choice, and not just because he wanted her to sell out Grawk. She probably *should* do that because she couldn't let any more harm come to Sophie T. – but what then? She knew Beard and Spike would never let them go, no matter how much she cooperated.

"Look," said another voice, calm and reasonable. "You're doing this all wrong."

"I beg your pardon?" Beard growled, eyebrows raised in disbelief. "Who asked you?"

"Oh, no one," said Charlie. "Sorry to interrupt.

 115

I was just trying to help."

Sophie T. swung her legs ferociously in Beard's other hand, and Amelia stared at Charlie.

"What would you do, then?" said Spike.

"Well," said Charlie, "it seems as though you've all forgotten about the wormhole you need to catch."

Spike gaped at him, and then turned to Beard. "How long do we have?"

Beard grunted in grudging agreement. "We are cutting it fine."

"Right," said Charlie. "So wouldn't you be better off setting your trap near the gateway? If you're depending on Grawk to come to you anyway ..."

Beard snorted. "And what do you expect to get out of this *help* you're giving us?"

Amelia swiveled her eyes to see Charlie standing below her. He looked tiny beside the giants but shrugged and sighed as if not particularly upset with the way things were turning out.

"Look," he said. "Amelia there is a good person – she really cares about what's right and wrong, and she's never going to change. But me? Well, I'm much more practical. I can see you're going to win in the end no matter what we do, so I figure: why not make it a bit easier for myself?"

Beard laughed. "Oh, there's a pirate heart in the boy! Well done, lad – I like your thinking. Lead on. We'll take the bait to the gateway as you suggest."

"Me?" said Charlie. "Oh, sorry – I can't do that. I'm totally lost out here. I was hoping you remembered the way back."

Spike snorted. "A pirate heart, maybe, but no brain to go with it. Fine. You follow me, then."

Spike slung both giant backpacks over his shoulders and strode out of the clearing, his plasma gun at the ready, with Foxy and Charlie jogging along to keep up. Beard brought up the rear, Amelia and Sophie T. clamped awkwardly under his arms.

Amelia thought she understood what Charlie was doing. She hoped she did, anyway. Once or twice, she thought she saw a faint yellow glow through the bushes. Perhaps Charlie had seen it too.

It was a strange experience being carried through the bush, like flying six feet above the ground, only much more uncomfortable and with a lot of branches and leaves whipping across her face. She wondered how Sophie T. was coping with it.

They made rapid progress. Even though Charlie and Foxy's legs were so much shorter, Spike didn't slow for them, and in a few minutes Amelia thought she recognized the land. Surely

Lady Naomi's work station was over that way?

And then it was obvious that they were close to the headland. Between the trees, Amelia glimpsed open ground and in the distance, the lights of the hotel itself. The ground dipped away here, and Spike led them into a narrow trench between two massive slabs of rock. This wasn't the way they'd come into the bush, but Amelia had been here before, weeks ago, when she'd been exploring with Charlie. This fissure between the rocks went on for ten feet or more, going around a couple of sharps bends, almost as perfect a labyrinth as the hedge maze.

The black silhouette perched on the crest of one rock was new, though. Amelia blinked, and it was gone. She could almost have imagined it.

Spike followed the path around the first corner, disappeared from view, and there was a heavy thump. Then silence.

Beard stopped dead and called out in his own language. There was no reply. "You," he said to Foxy. "Go and see."

"Me?" Foxy quailed. "No, not me, I – oh, send the boy."

"Me?" said Charlie. "On my own? Are you crazy?" But he flicked a look Amelia's way, and her heart beat faster.

"*Do it*," said Beard. When Charlie opened his mouth to protest, he said again, "Do it," and shook Amelia and Sophie T. at him for emphasis.

Amelia didn't know how much more of this throttling she could take. Whatever was going to happen to them, she wished it would just hurry up and happen.

Charlie heaved a sigh, pushed past Foxy, and rather nervously picked his way around the edge of the rock wall. Amelia saw him pause for a second before his disappeared behind it, and then – nothing.

"Boy!" shouted Beard. "What's going on?"

There was a flash of light reflected on the rocks – as if Spike's plasma gun had been fired – and then: more nothing.

"Boy!" Beard called again, more uncertain this time. Then he barked at Foxy, "Now you look."

"Not a chance! Who knows what's around that corner?"

"Well, you would, useless, if you used that scanner of yours."

"Oh. Right." Foxy adjusted the controls and then, very reluctantly, approached the turn in the path. "Oh, my."

"What?" said Beard. "Is my brother still there? Is he alive?"

"Hm?" Foxy looked up. "Oh, yes, he's there. And alive. The human, too."

"So what's the problem?"

"Ah …" Foxy stalled as if unsure of how to say it. Or unwilling. "I think …" He looked up, but couldn't quite meet Beard's eyes. In fact, Amelia thought he was looking at *her* when he said, "I think you'd better check it out yourself."

Beard grumbled, but put Amelia and Sophie T. down at last. Both girls crumpled to the ground. Amelia's legs were all pins and needles.

"Look after these two," he ordered Foxy. "And if they get away, it'll be taken out of your pay." Drawing his net gun, he glided along the path to the corner. It was spooky how quietly he moved. Amelia put her arm around Sophie T. and watched as the alien stepped briskly around the corner, his gun held out in front of him, ready to fire.

Before he could, though, a bolt of plasma caught him square in the chest. Sophie T. flinched as he instantly locked solid and fell back with a ghastly, meaty sound against the rock behind him.

He stayed propped there, like a ladder leaning against a wall, petrified.

What now? Amelia thought, but Foxy was already skipping ahead, calling, "Well done! Such quick think–"

He stopped abruptly and gulped.

Amelia stood up. "Charlie?"

"All good," came his cheerful reply.

She didn't bother with words then, but ran to stand beside Foxy. There, on the path beyond the blind corner, was Charlie. He was grinning with Spike's colossal plasma gun in both hands. Spike was on the ground, his hands raised to shield his face, and had clearly been petrified too. Standing guard over him was Grawk, and Grawk was now staring at the shivering Foxy.

Amelia clapped. "Charlie! You did this?"

"It was Grawk, mostly," he said modestly. "He's not the Hulk, Amelia – he's Batman: silent,

brilliant, and out for revenge. He ambushed Spike by himself, and when I came around, all I had to do was get his gun and shoot him while Grawk pretended he was about to eat him. At least," he looked at Grawk, "I *think* he was only pretending."

"Thanks, Grawk," said Amelia, feeling oddly shy. Grawk wagged his tail slightly, though his gaze never wavered from Foxy. "And thanks, Charlie. I wasn't sure what you were up to at first."

"Neither was I," he admitted. "Hey, but where's Sophie T.?"

"I'm here," said a tiny voice.

"Oh, hey, Soph!" Charlie said happily. "Glad you're all right. And look – we found Grawk!"

"Excuse me," said Foxy, hardly daring to move his lips. "What about me?"

"Right," said Amelia, stepping back to Beard's petrified body and pulling his gun from his hand.

"Well, why don't you explain to Grawk how you were only trying to help him. We'll let him decide if he agrees. And while you're doing that, I'm going to shoot these two guys with the binding gun."

Sophie T. made a small noise of distress and put her hand on Amelia's arm.

"Oh, sorry, Soph," said Amelia, immediately contrite. "I'm being so rude. *You're* the guest – would you like to shoot the bad guys instead?"

CHAPTER TEN

Walking back onto the hotel grounds, the moon was bright and indifferent above them as Charlie tried to help Sophie T. look on the bright side.

"I know the last part was a bit rough," he said, "but at least you were totally unconscious for most of it."

"No, I wasn't," she retorted.

"Yeah, with the petrifying ray and stuff. You weren't aware of anything then."

"I was paralyzed, Charles, not asleep."

"You mean –"

"I saw and heard and felt *every*thing. And it was the worst experience in the world."

"Oh, no ..." Charlie groaned.

"Yes, that's awful," said Amelia. "You must have been so frightened."

"No," Charlie said. "Not that – but, Tom saw me look under his eye patch!"

"Ugh, Charlie," Amelia scolded, and shoved him in the shoulder.

"So, what do we do now?" Sophie T. asked, a little cautiously. "I mean, what do we say to your parents?"

"Ah," Amelia grimaced. "About that ... you see, they sort of ..." There was no way around it. "They know everything. About aliens and stuff."

Sophie T. goggled at them both, then turned to stare back at Foxy behind them, and Grawk who was walking very closely behind him, escorting the miserable scientist as his prisoner. "So," she said slowly, "this isn't the first time this sort of thing has happened to you."

"No," said Charlie.

"You knew there were aliens all this time?"

"Yes," said Amelia.

"And you still invited me for a sleepover!"

"Well," Amelia didn't know the right answer to that. "It was my birthday ... and I really like you ... and ..."

"Plus, we had no idea this was going to happen," Charlie finished. "Amelia only planned the cake, pizza, and movie parts."

Sophie T. shuddered and crossed her arms tightly.

"Sophie?" Amelia said gently.

Sophie T. didn't answer.

"Well, she asked the right question, anyway," said Charlie. "What do we do now? Go back to the hotel?"

Amelia looked up the hill and imagined her bed still warm and waiting for her. "No," she sighed. "We'd better go down to Tom's with Grawk and Foxy."

"But what about –" He nodded at Sophie T.

Amelia shrugged. "It's a bit late to worry about secrets now."

To their relief, all the lights were on in Tom's cottage when they arrived, and it was full of people. Tom was sitting up with a mug of black tea between his hands, the crocheted blanket still around his shoulders, and glowering. Mum was on the phone (the cord clumsily repaired with electrical tape) and asking impatient questions, and James was poring over a stack of reorganized charts. Mary was in the kitchen, closest to the front door, and so the first person to see them arrive. "They're alive!" she gasped, waving across the room to get the others' attention.

"As usual," said Charlie, squirming to get away as his mum swooped in to try to kiss him.

"Oh, thank goodness," cried Mum, ignoring the muffled voice coming out of the phone. "If only there was some way to let Dad and Lady Naomi know you're safe."

"Guess what?" said Amelia. "We've got Grawk back. He saved us again."

"Where is he?" James asked.

"Grawk?" Amelia called.

Foxy came in first, cowering a bit.

"You!" said Mum, slamming down the phone.

Grawk padded in after him, and everyone sucked in a breath, shocked.

"Did you do this to him?" Mum asked Foxy.

"No!"

"It's true," said Amelia. "Grawk was like this

when we first saw him. It's because he's growing up on Earth, or something."

Mum and Tom swapped anxious looks.

"Amelia ..."

"It's not his fault," she said, and without thinking she stepped close to him and laid a protective hand on his neck. As her fingers sank into his velvety fur, she realized this was the first time she'd touched him since before he'd disappeared. And from the looks on everyone's faces, they were just as uncertain of Grawk as she was. True, he'd defended them from harm, and she was sure he was still basically good, but did that mean he was *safe*? Maybe not.

She felt him vibrating under her hand, and when she heard the deep grinding noise, she nearly snatched it away. Then she recognized that this was his purr, not his growl, and she dared to scratch him behind the jaw.

"See?" she said, trying to sound more positive than she felt. "It's still Grawk. He's just bigger."

"We're going to have to tell Ms. Rosby," said Mum.

"Oh, but –"

"She's already on her way," Mum spoke over her. "As soon as we saw that your beds were empty, Dad called Tom. And then, with his line being cut, we knew there was trouble. Lady Naomi had heard a scream, and she and Dad went out to see if they could find where you'd gone. That just left me and Mary in the hotel, so of course we called Control. At the very least," she smiled sadly at Sophie T., "we have to own up to letting one more person into the gateway club."

Sophie T. looked warily at all the faces suddenly turned to her. Amelia felt thoroughly bad for her. Sophie T. had been so worried about being laughed at, but they'd done worse than that –

they'd lied to her. And for all her fears of being left out, now she was stuck on the inside of a secret she'd never wanted to know.

James seemed to recognize what Sophie T. was going through. "Come on," he said, getting up from the charts and coming over to put a hand on her shoulder. "I'll make you some really sweet tea and you can ask me anything you like until this starts to make sense to you."

Sophie T. nodded forlornly and followed him to Tom's kitchen. "I don't think this will ever make sense."

"Maybe not," James admitted. "But after a while, your brain will sort of stretch enough to fit it in. You'll see."

"I doubt it," said Sophie T., tiptoeing past Grawk with a little shudder. But when she got to the kitchen, Mary wrapped her up in a huge motherly hug, and fussed over her.

"Oh, you poor child, oh, *manari mou*, come and tell me all about it."

Charlie rolled his eyes in sympathy, but Amelia saw Sophie T. snuggle deeper into Mary's arms, and thought Sophie T. was in just the right place.

"As for you," Mum said to Foxy, "you're under house arrest until Ms. Rosby gets here."

Foxy huffed at the news, but didn't look too sorry to be taken out of Grawk's custody.

She handcuffed Foxy's wrist to the leg of Tom's desk, and then turned to Amelia. "We really are going to have to do something about Grawk, cookie."

Amelia stood closer still to the warm black body, amazed at both his familiarity (his smell, the softness of his fur) and his newness (he sat down, and his head was now level with Amelia's), but determined not to let her doubts show.

"Mum, without Grawk we all would have

been killed, captured or lost in a repeating time bubble about six times already. We don't need to do anything about him. We should just be glad we've got him."

"I am," said Mum. "I'm grateful to him every day, and I know he's kept us safe ever since he got here. But how long can we keep *him* safe? How big will he eventually grow? And how will we – no, don't worry about keeping him secret – how will we even keep him *fed?*"

"I don't know." Amelia had never felt so miserable so soon after surviving an adventure.

"Yes!" said Mary, at the mention of feeding. "These children have been out all night – they must be starving. Let's take them back to the hotel so I can get something warm into this little bird." She gave Sophie T. a protective squeeze, and Sophie T. smiled shyly.

"Oh, that's nice," said Charlie. "What about

Amelia and me? Aren't we little birds, too?"

Mary grumbled at him in Greek, and Charlie laughed in reply.

"Hang on," said James. "Aren't we forgetting something? Was this guy," he pointed at Foxy, "the only alien out there tonight?"

Sophie T. shivered, and Amelia said, "No, there were some other guys, but trust us: they're not going anywhere."

"Stunned and netted," Charlie nodded. "And Foxy was nice enough to show us how to turn the guns up to maximum, so we know they won't escape."

"OK," said Mum, looking a little stunned herself at the answer, but happy enough to accept it. "Mary's right. Tom, if you're OK babysitting this fellow, we'll take the kids back up to bed. And –" she added quickly, as Charlie opened his mouth to protest "– get them something to eat."

Heading out of the cottage, Amelia and Charlie walked with Sophie T., one on either side of her, just in case she still felt bothered by the dark, even with Grawk, James and two mums with them.

"I really am sorry," Amelia said again. "I promise you, tonight wasn't on purpose."

"And I'm sorry about my mum," said Charlie. "She can be such a pain."

To Amelia's surprise, Sophie T. giggled. "You should have heard what she said about *you*, Charles."

"Huh?"

"In the kitchen," Sophie T. went on, sounding quite pleased with herself. "She told me you were the naughtiest, most disobedient, reckless boy she'd ever met in her life, and it would serve you right if you ended up eaten by space monsters one day."

"That traitor!" Charlie yelped. "My own mother! Well, I suppose you loved hearing that even my mum agrees with you that I'm a fool."

"But I don't agree with her," said Sophie T.

Charlie's jaw dropped.

Sophie T. went on, "I told her you were very smart and very brave and it wasn't just Grawk who saved us. You did too, Charlie."

He gaped at her. Amelia couldn't believe what she was hearing either.

"Seriously?" he asked. "I thought you thought I was silly."

Sophie T. snorted and tossed back her hair. "Oh, Charles, you really don't know anything, do you?"

Cerberus Jones

Cerberus Jones is the three-headed writing team made up of Chris Morphew, Rowan McAuley and David Harding.

Chris Morphew is *The Gateway's* story architect. Chris's experience writing adventures for *Zac Power* and heart-stopping twists for *The Phoenix Files* makes him the perfect man for the job!

Rowan McAuley is the team's chief writer. Before joining Cerberus Jones, Rowan wrote some of the most memorable stories and characters in the best-selling *Go Girl!* series.

David Harding's job is editing and continuity. He is also the man behind *Robert Irwin's Dinosaur Hunter* series, as well as several *RSPCA Animal Tales* titles.